THE PICNIC CAPER

written by Carol Reinsma
pictures by Nathan Cori

STANDARD
PUBLISHING

The Standard Publishing Company, Cincinnati, Ohio
A division of Standex International Corporation
© 1994 by The Standard Publishing Company
All rights reserved.
Printed in the United States of America
01 00 99 98 97 96 95 94   5 4 3 2 1

Library of Congress Catalog Card Number 93-29567
ISBN 0-7847-0006-0
Cataloging-in-Publication data available

Edited by Diane Stortz
Designed by Coleen Davis

CONTENTS

A Happy Start

On Saturday,

Locust hopped to the park

for the Hopper Day picnic.

Grasshopper, Treehopper,

and hoppers

of all kinds came, too.

At the park, loud and sharp noises

came from under the big tent.

Hoppers screeched on violins.

They banged on drums

and blew on horns.

Locust covered her ears.

And so did the rest of the crowd.

"That band needs a leader,"
said Locust.
Grasshopper sprang over
to Locust and whispered
in her ear.
"No way," said Locust.

"Please," said Grasshopper.

"You can do it. I know you can."

Locust stood tall.

"See, I am too small," said Locust.

"But I know you can do it,"

said Grasshopper.

So Locust stood in front

of the noisy band.

The band players put down

their violins, drums, and horns.

Then Treehopper yelled,
"*That* little hopper
cannot help.
She is too little.
What a lulu!"

Locust put her head down.

"Do not listen to Treehopper,"

said Grasshopper.

"You can do it.

I know you can."

"Lulu!" yelled Treehopper.

But Locust looked at the band.

She thought about

Grasshopper's words.

She saw a stick on the ground

and picked it up.

11

Locust waved the stick
and counted, "One, two, three."
All the hoppers in the band
played together, one, two, three.
Sweet and lively music
filled the tent. Hoppers
sang and skipped.

It was a perfect start

for the Hopper Day picnic.

A good person's words will help many others.
Proverbs 10:21

The Bean Bag Toss

The games started at ten o'clock.

Locust tossed a bean bag

at the target.

She missed.

Treehopper laughed
and said to Grasshopper,
"It is fun to see
someone miss."
But to Locust she called,
"Good throw, Lulu!"

Locust tossed another bean bag.

She missed again.

But Treehopper yelled,

"What a toss!"

So Locust smiled and

threw another bean bag.

She missed again.

16

Cockroach came to watch.

She put her picnic basket

on the grass.

"Keep your eye on the target,"

said Cockroach.

"Treehopper says

my throws are good," said Locust.

"But you could hit the target
if you looked at it,"
said Cockroach.
Locust stomped her left foot
and threw another bean bag.
She missed again.

Treehopper laughed.

"What a good miss —

I mean good throw," she said.

"Maybe Cockroach is right,"

said Locust.

Locust looked at the target.

She threw another bean bag.

The bean bag hit the target.

"Hurrah!" shouted Locust.

She shook Cockroach's hand

for a long time.

"Join me for lunch," said Cockroach.

Green cheese

and brown banana peels

spilled out of Cockroach's basket.

"Thank you for inviting me,"
said Locust.
"But let's share my lunch instead."
Locust opened her lunch.
Cockroach smacked her lips.

So under the shade of a big sunflower, they ate golden cheese and fresh apples.

Those who correct others will later be liked more than those who give false praise.
Proverbs 28:23

Log Hop

"Let's play log hop," said Locust.

"Good idea," said Grasshopper.

Treehopper jumped on their log.

"May I play?" she asked.

"Yes," said Grasshopper.

"But first help us move the stones

away from the logs.

Then we must bring in sand

for a soft landing."

"I will come back

when you are

ready to play,"

said Treehopper.

"We need your help

to get ready," said Locust.

Locust moved stones.

Grasshopper put sand

beside each log.

But Treehopper sat in the shade.

"Hey, Lulu," she said.

"You forgot to move a stone.

Grassy, you need more sand."

Locust and Grasshopper

kept working.

"It is hot,"

complained Treehopper.

"I am going to get a drink."

Treehopper left.

Locust and Grasshopper

kept working.

Finally Treehopper came back.

Locust and Grasshopper

were still working.

"Are we ready for log hop yet?"

asked Treehopper.

"I have been waiting for hours.

I want some fun."

Locust and Grasshopper

stopped working.

"I am quitting," said Locust.

"Me, too," said Grasshopper.

"You are no fun," said Treehopper.

"A little work

and you are ready to quit."

"No," said Grasshopper.

"We are not tired from work."

"What is the problem then?"

asked Treehopper.

"*You* are the problem,"

said Grasshopper.

"We are tired

of your complaining,"

said Locust.

Locust and Grasshopper
sat on the log.
Treehopper sprang into the air
and disappeared.
"Grassy and Lulu
are lazy, no-good friends,"
she said.

When Treehopper was gone,
Locust and Grasshopper
played game after game
of log hop.

Stone is heavy, and sand is hard to carry.
But the complaining of a foolish person
causes more trouble than either.
Proverbs 27:3

33

A Better Joke

Locust stretched

and rubbed her back legs.

"I am ready to hop

in the long race," she said.

"Every hopper who finishes

before three o'clock is a winner."

"You can do it,"

said Grasshopper.

"I know you can."

The race began.

Locust worked hard

and hopped high

above the grass.

Suddenly, Treehopper

hopped beside Locust.

"You look tired,"

said Treehopper.

"I am tired," said Locust.

"But I can make it."

"I have an idea,"

said Treehopper.

"Take this path.

It is a shortcut."

"No," said Locust.

"Please take the shortcut,"

said Treehopper.

"I want to make up

for not helping you

with the log hop."

Treehopper looked sad.

"Well," said Locust,

"I do want to be a winner."

So she hopped down the path.

At three o'clock
all the hoppers
were at the finish line,
except for Locust.

At four o'clock,

Locust still was not there.

"Something terrible

must have happened,"

said Grasshopper.

41

"Don't blame me,"
said Treehopper.
"The shortcut
I told her about
was just a joke."
All the hoppers
looked at Treehopper.
"What have you done?"
asked Grasshopper.

"I told her to take
a shortcut," said Treehopper.
"She should be here soon."
"Locust may be lost forever!"
cried Grasshopper.

Finally Locust reached

the finish line.

She was dripping wet.

"I fell into the river,"

said Locust.

"I tricked you," said Treehopper.

"I was wrong. Please forgive me."

"Don't forgive *her*,"

said Grasshopper.

"I think Treehopper

is sorry this time,"

said Locust.

"I forgive you, Treehopper."

"Thank you!" said Treehopper.

"Great!" said Locust.

"Does this mean

you will not forget my name

and call me Lulu?"

"I will call you Locust,"

said Treehopper.

"Knock, knock," said Locust.

"Who is there?" asked Treehopper.

"You forgot my name!" said

Locust. Treehopper and Locust

fell down laughing together.

A person shouldn't trick his neighbor
and then say, "I was just joking."
Proverbs 26:18